FEDERICO EXAGGERATE

Written by Hazel Pacheco
Illustrated by Kim Sponaugle

A STORY ABOUT TALL TALES, HONESTY,
AND . . . THE BOLDEST BERRY!

Henry and Friends Book 2

"Bear with each other and forgive one another if any of you has a grievance against someone. ..." ~ Colossians 3:13

Dedication

For all Little Free Library Stewards who treat us to adventures through the books they share.

Thank you to . . .

my family and friends who are my unconditional supporters;
my Aunt Cecilia who suggested including a glossary;
my editor extraordinaire, Nevin Mays, the unsung heroine of this process; and,
my cover designer and illustrator, Kim Sponaugle, the architect of imagination.

Other Books by Hazel Pacheco

That's How It Was: Operation Finders Keepers
Henry Wondered
Gloria Smiled (coming soon)
Ernesto Joked (coming soon)

Copyright

Pajarito Chronicles

Federico was a fantastic storyteller! Actually . . . Federico exaggerated a lot!

One morning, he was treating the covey to yet another wild tale.

"Flash! Craaack! Ka-BOOM!"

"There I was during a monster thunderstorm, smack dab in the middle of an angry river," he crowed, referring to the Rio Grande (ree-oh-grahn-day). "Suddenly, the log I was riding was ripped away by crashing waves!"

Gloria smiled and said, "Oh my!"

"Way to go with the flow!" joked Ernesto.

Henry wondered why Gloria smiled. They lived in a cottonwood forest called the bosque (boss-kee). Quails in the bosque don't swim.

Just then, an alert sounded. **"Kree kreee!"**

Federico's audience turned their attention to Clara.

She announced, "A sagebrush sparrow tweeted there are ripe hackberries just north of——"

The covey started a stampede north before Clara could finish.

Federico planted his feet and shouted, "**Stop!** I haven't gotten to the best part!"

Gloria pleaded, "Tell us on the way. The hackberries will be gone if we don't hurry."

"Can't you hear the berries calling our names?" Henry asked.

Federico listened—he didn't hear his name. All he could hear was the faint thunder of birds racing north.

Ernesto called, "I don't want to miss out. I'm hungry! *Seed* you later!"

Alone, Federico stomped off in the opposite direction. "I bet those berries are too sour for a robin," he muttered. "I bet those berries are too small for an ant."

Scurrying through the bosque, past the cottonwood trees, Federico stumbled and went down with a thud. His feet were tangled in vines. Dazed, he picked himself up . . . then he pinched himself. No——he wasn't dreaming.

Before him were huge green berries—each one the
size of a small boulder! He followed a trail of ants to a
berry that was cracked. The inside was bright red.
Federico imagined wild strawberries and drooled.

He drilled into the outer rind like a yellow-bellied sapsucker. The inside was cool, sweet, fruity, and . . . sprinkled with seeds! The combination made his tastebuds dance.

Federico stopped, cocked his head, and thought,

"I could be a **legend!**"

He tried pulling
one of the smaller berries,
"Hrrmph!"

Then, he tried
pushing it,
"Umph!"
It wouldn't budge.
Wiping his forehead,
he had another idea.

Federico raced back at roadrunner speed.

He spotted the covey, scrambled to the top of an old tree stump, and crowed,

"Berries! Huge! GINORMOUS!"

But there was no excitement. No hoopla. Only a few eye rolls. Even his best friends continued to hunt for seeds.

Hopping down from the stump, Federico asked
Ernesto, "Any hackberries?"

"Only the early birds get the hackberries," mumbled
Ernesto.

Henry and Gloria nodded.

Federico studied his feet, then looked at the covey. In a quiet but urgent voice, he said, "Honest. I found berries that taste better than nectar. They're sprinkled with seeds, *and* they're too heavy to push or pull!"

Tummies rumbling, the covey looked from Federico to Henry.

Henry pursed his beak and narrowed his eyes, then he noticed something.

"What's on your wing?" he asked Federico.

Federico preened his feathers and exclaimed,
"Berry seeds! Look!"

Henry rubbed his forehead. Then looking at his
friend, he sighed and said, "Lead the way."

Puffing up his chest, Federico scurried back to the berry patch
with the covey following.

Once there, Federico presented his find with a dramatic swoosh of his wings and a crow of "ta-da!" Looking at the group and seeing ovals where beaks should be, he added, "Told you!" They all started to laugh. What else could they do?

Have a fiesta of course!

The fiesta (fee-eh-stuh) or celebration included lots of slurping and munching while Federico treated the covey to his fantastic true tale about how he discovered The Boldest Berry.

A story he'd tell over, and over, and over again. And that's no exaggeration!

Just In Case You Wondered . . .

bosque (boss-kee) — Spanish word for forest; a small area of trees or brush along the riverbanks in the southwestern part of the United States

cottonwood trees - large trees found in the bosque along the Rio Grande; their cotton-like seeds float in the breeze

covey — a community of quails

fiesta (fee-eh-stuh) — Spanish word for celebration

hackberry — a sweet purple berry with a small nut inside; grows on trees

nectar — a sweet liquid produced by fruits, and flowers

preen — bird behavior: to clean and smooth feathers

quail — a sociable small bird that rarely flies

Rio Grande (ree-oh grahn-day) — Spanish for big river; a river that begins in Colorado and flows through New Mexico to the Gulf of Mexico

roadrunner — a bird known for its land speed

robin — a songbird with a red belly; known to have an appetite for sour berries no matter how bitter

sagebrush sparrow — a songbird with a long tail; known for perching up high when it sings

yellow-bellied sapsucker — a small woodpecker with a yellow belly that drills holes in trees for its sap

Just for Fun

Identify the items below from smallest to largest?

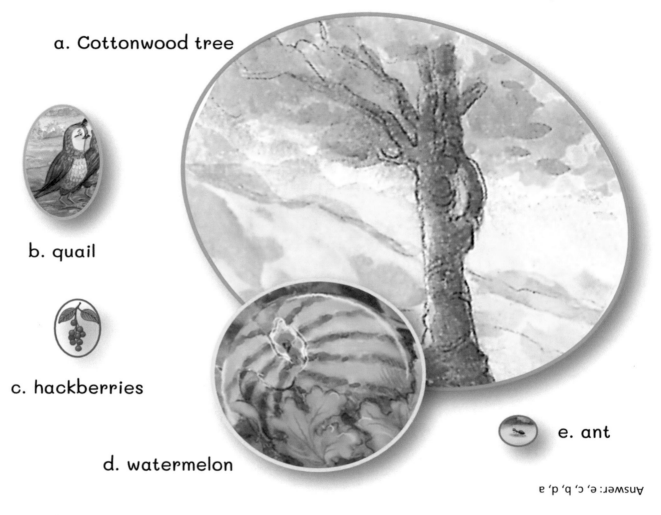

a. Cottonwood tree

b. quail

c. hackberries

d. watermelon

e. ant

Trivia: Which of the birds listed below is known for its land speed?

a. yellow-bellied sapsucker b. robin c. roadrunner d. sagebrush sparrow

About the Editor: Nevin Mays is a children's book addict, dog editor and chocolate cuddler... and sometimes makes embarrassing malapropisms! As a freelancer editor, she helps authors and publishers create and polish picture books, chapter books, and novels for kids and teens. She has experience in many mediums, including audiobooks, interactive ebooks, and novelty books. You can find her at www.nevinmays.com.

About the Illustrator: Kim Sponaugle uses her God-given talent to leave a mark on the heart. Her style can be described as render-based traditional, using vibrant watercolor. Her strength is in creating emotion through action. Her art converges somewhere in the sweet spot of whimsy where realistic and cartoon meet. You can find her at www.picturekitchenstudio.com.

Author's Note: Many people know New Mexico for our chile, but there are a number of farms along the Rio Grande bosque that grow watermelon. When doing research for this book, I was surprised to learn a watermelon is a berry!

Thank you for reading *Federico Exaggerated.* I hope it made you smile and want to share it with your family and friends. Your feedback is important, so I hope you take time to post a review.

Henry and Friends Series

Henry Wondered. A Story About Jealousy, Serendipity and . . . Flamenco!
Book one of the Henry and Friends Series

Federico Exaggerated. A Story About Tall Tales, Honesty, and . . . The Boldest Berry!
Book two of the Henry and Friends Series

Gloria Smiled. A Story About Disappointment, Resilience, and . . . The Sorpresa!
Book three of the Henry and Friends Series

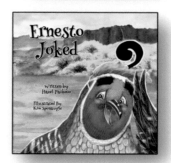

Ernesto Joked. A Story About Humor, Courage, and . . . Señor Coyote!
Book four of the Henry and Friends Series

Ever wish you could capture your parent's childhood memories?

This is a tribute to childhood back when...

Made in United States
Troutdale, OR
12/08/2023

15356618R00017